WHEN THE TRUCK GOT STUCK!

JOY COWLEY

illustrated by Jenny Cooper

Learning Media

CHAPTER 1

Every day after school, Antwan Cuff sat outside his house high above the freeway. Far below, the traffic went by like rows of shining bugs – cars and pickups, vans and buses, motorcycles and fire engines.

Best of all, Antwan liked the big rigs
with their roaring engines and
thundering wheels. When he was old
enough, he would have his own rig.
Until then, he could watch the trucks
and drive them in his dreams.

One day, a new rig came roaring off the
freeway and onto the little road that led
to the town of Woodchuck. The rig was
high and wide. Antwan could just see
the words "ice cream" on the side and a
picture of an ice-cream cone.

But why was the truck on *that* road?

Antwan knew that further on there was a low concrete bridge over the Woodchuck road. He held his breath and waited.

He heard the rig change gears. There
was a squealing sound of metal scraping
on concrete. The noise went on and on.
Then it stopped. Antwan jumped up,
trying to see past the trees.

Yes! The truck was stuck!

CHAPTER 2

Under the bridge, the driver got out of the rig and scratched his head. "Uh-oh!" he muttered. "Looks like I'm stuck."

A tanker pulled up behind him. "Have *you* got a problem!" said the tanker driver. "Don't worry. I'll push you. You'll be out of there in two shakes of a hound dog's tail."

The tanker driver drove up against the truck. She pushed and pushed. Some crumbs of concrete fell down from the bridge, but the truck did not move.

The tanker driver said, "It's OK. I've got my phone. I'll call a tow truck from Woodchuck. It should be able to pull you out."

"Thanks! You're a pal," said the truck driver.

CHAPTER 3

A tow truck with chains came from Woodchuck.

"Stuck, are you?" said the tow truck driver. "Don't worry, man! I'll have you out of there before you can say *Yankee Doodle!*"

They hooked the chains up to the ice-cream truck, and the tow truck pulled and pulled. More bits of concrete fell, but the truck did not move.

The driver of the ice-cream truck didn't know what to do next. He couldn't go forward. He couldn't go back. Traffic was backing up behind him. If he stayed much longer, there would be a major traffic jam and his load of ice cream would melt.

The tanker driver had her phone ready. "We'll have to call the highway patrol," she said.

CHAPTER 4

So much traffic had stopped on the Woodchuck road that the highway patrol officers had to leave their car on the main highway and walk to the bridge.

The officers walked around the ice-cream truck shaking their heads. One of them said, "This truck is as stuck as a cork in a bottle. There's nothing we can do. Better call the bridge engineer."

Soon, a helicopter landed in a nearby
field, and the bridge engineer got out.
He was tired and hot and grumpy. He
wished he were back at home, watching
the game on TV.

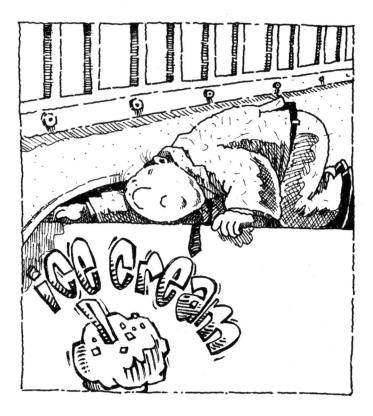

Huffing and puffing, the bridge engineer climbed on top of the rig and looked at the bridge. "There's only one thing to be done," he said. "Get a welding torch and cut the top off the truck."

"No way!" said the truck driver.

"Nobody is cutting my beautiful new rig. Bring in some concrete drills and take the bottom off the bridge."

"Definitely not," said the engineer. "We can't weaken the bridge. Your truck is the problem. It's too high!"

"Your bridge is to blame. It's too low!"

"Nonsense!" shouted the engineer. "Cut the top off the truck."

"Over my dead body!" yelled the truck driver. "Do something about that bridge."

CHAPTER 5

The Woodchuck road was filled with noise. The engineer argued with the truck driver. The truck driver argued with the engineer. Behind them, the people in their cars were tired of waiting. They tooted their horns and yelled out of their windows, "We want to go home!"

At last, Antwan Cuff reached the little
bridge. He walked out on to the concrete
span and looked down at the truck.
"Excuse me, sir," he said to the driver.
"This truck is stopping
the traffic."

"Beat it, kid!" growled the driver. "Go home and tell your mother she needs you."

Antwan pointed to the back of the truck. "But you've got ice cream in there. It's going to melt all over the road. If I were you, I'd move this rig."

"Would you now!" said the driver. He put his hands on his hips and glared at Antwan. "And just how would you do that?"

Antwan Cuff smiled. "Well, sir," he said.
"I'd let some air out of the tires."

The truck driver looked at the bridge engineer. The bridge engineer looked at the truck driver.

The highway patrol officers and the tow truck driver and the tanker driver all smiled and looked at their feet.

"Oh!" everyone said.

CHAPTER 6

Air hissed out of the big rig's tires. The wheels settled closer to the road, and a gap appeared between the top of the truck and the bottom of the bridge.

The truck driver said to Antwan, "Son, I reckon you've earned yourself a reward."

Ten minutes later, the traffic was on its way and the truck driver was unloading ice cream at the Woodchuck store.

Antwan Cuff was also on his way,
carrying a big carton and running as fast
as he could.

He wanted to get home before that ice cream melted!